PUMA DREAMS

Written by TONY JOHNSTON   Illustrated by JIM LAMARCHE

A PAULA WISEMAN BOOK
Simon & Schuster Books for Young Readers
New York   London   Toronto   Sydney   New Delhi

My gram says everybody needs
at least one dream.
Mine is to see a puma.
Gram calls that a long-dream
for it may not ever happen.
She says pumas are elusive
as a handful of wind.

That their numbers are dwindling,
getting smaller and smaller.
Some are hunted down.
Some are forced from the land
when people move in.
So they keep shy of people
and to themselves.
Quiet. Like secrets.

Near here, years ago,
a puma showed up by a horse corral,
stalking supper.
And somebody spotted one
down our canyon,
dozing on an old oak limb.
A neighbor says puma kittens
once were hiding in his barn.
But me, I've never seen one.
I want to—before they are gone.

It is summer now.
The grass is dry.
The hills are puma-colored.
This time of year
my dream wakes up
and roams my mind.
I make a plan.
Animals love the tang of salt,
like kids love sweet.
I'll place a salt lick on a hill
close to our house,
where I can watch it.
"Till the cows come home."
That's a saying of Gram's.
I'll fix on that salt lick
when I can. I hope
if I'm patient and a little lucky,
I'll see my puma.

One damp morning
fog swallows the hills
and creeps through the trees,
slow and thick, like a mystery.
Gram and I jounce down
to the feed barn in her old truck.
I invest my allowance money
in a salt lick.
Fifty pounds. Like me.
We jounce back and struggle
the salt from the pickup. *Plunk!*
Then we grin at each other
and lick it, for luck.

Now I wait—for a puma.
It may take days, years,
or never. But you don't give up
on dreams, Gram says. "Easy dreams
aren't worth a pin or a pickle."

I watch for a puma
to come to the salt lick.
I imagine that big cat
slipping through our wheat field
on whisper-feet.
Slow, oh slow. Like fog.
But I never see one.

I imagine it as it prowls
the dark. With owls.
But I never see one.
I imagine snow dusting my puma
as it hunts in the darkest hours.
Still no luck.

Days go by. Months.
Other animals come and mark
the lick with their tongues—
deer, cattle, elk.
Finches sign it
with their tiny beaks.
And roadrunners, who enjoy
admiring themselves in the mirrors
of Gram's truck.

A small rain turns our road to mud.
When it dries I *almost* see a puma.
There are cat tracks there—
as big as hands.
My dream is close, but far.

I make myself a puma stick,
for when Gram and I walk the hills.
I whittle a small puma for a handle.
After many walks, from the rub
of my hand, the little puma
smooths and shines.

Time passes. And time.
Our salt lick is worn down
by many tongues.
But no puma's
that I have seen.
Gram says things happen
when you are looking the other way.

One early morning I am eating oatmeal,
my back to the salt-lick hill.
My skin begins to prickle.
Something is about to happen.
Something tells me to turn around.
So I do. Slowly.

And—there is my long-dream,
golden in the rising sun,
warily checking the salt.
It does not lick it,
just circles around it, head up.
Maybe sniffing to know
who has been there before.
Maybe to know who is still near.
I can't speak, so I just point.
Gram beams.
The puma is beautiful.
Partly because pumas may soon
disappear.
Partly because it just is.

When it goes away,
I keep looking at that place.
For me, the puma will always
glimmer there, a great golden ghost.

From the work of many tongues,
the salt sculpture is smaller now.
So I lug it home,
a doorstop for my room.
My gram says everybody needs
at least one dream.
My first one came true.
Soon a new dream takes its place.
I want to help pumas stay
in the world and be safe.
I don't know how to do that,
but I will find a way.

ABOUT THE PUMA

The puma is sometimes called "the ghost of the mountains" because it is so secretive. Other words to describe it are "shadowy," "wary," "aloof," "elusive," and "solitary." There are numerous names for the puma. Cougar, painter, panther, mountain lion, and Mexican lion are some. The Navajo call it *náshdóítsoh*.

After the jaguar, it is the second-largest cat of the Americas. A puma can grow to be six feet long and is the color of a lion. An ambush predator, one that sneaks up on its prey, it hunts mostly at night. Patience, silence, and stealth are keys to its success. Some believe that puma ancestors were so successful, they wiped out the ancient horses of the American continent.

Deer and elk are favorite prey, but a puma may attack smaller animals or livestock like sheep.

Pumas once ranged from North America to the Patagonia region of South America. Now they are endangered and can be seen mainly in national parks or other preserves. The problem is humans. People change the landscape with agriculture, home building, and other activities. So the puma's territory keeps shrinking. To survive, a puma avoids people as best it can, and so it is rarely seen.

Once when I was walking on a country road, a puma streaked in front of me, leaped into an oak, and disappeared. The memory of that beautiful wild creature was the beginning of this book.

If people protect them now, one day you might be lucky enough to see a puma in the wild.

There are many groups trying to protect the puma. You may want to contact one of them to learn more about this magnificent animal and to find out how you can help.

—T. J.

LIST OF GROUPS

The Cougar Fund: cougarfund.org

Mountain Lion Foundation: mountainlion.org/contributetakeaction.asp

National Geographic Big Cats Initiative: nationalgeographic.org/projects/big-cats-initiative

National Wildlife Federation Save LA Cougars Campaign: savelacougars.org

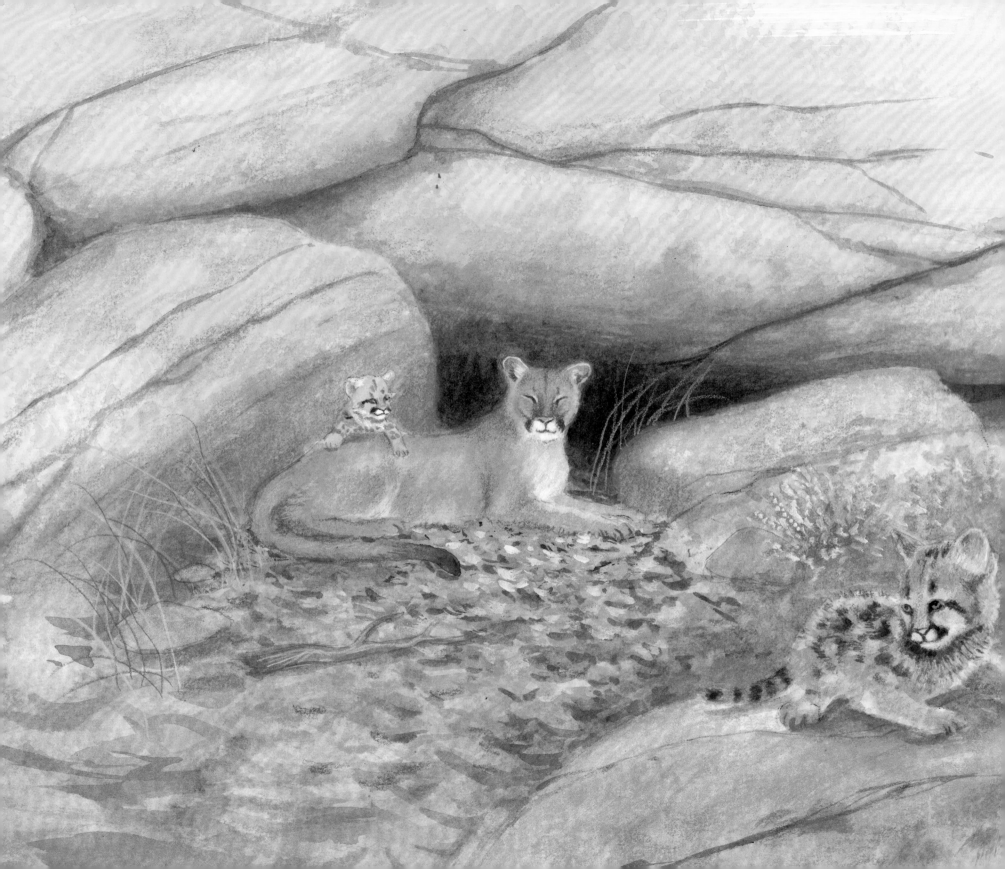

For Sue and Terry
and Mitch and Guy,
who know about pumas
—T. J.

For Kiera
—J. L.

SIMON & SCHUSTER BOOKS FOR YOUNG READERS

An imprint of Simon & Schuster Children's Publishing Division

1230 Avenue of the Americas, New York, New York 10020

Text copyright © 2019 by Johnston Family Trust • Illustrations copyright © 2019 by Jim LaMarche

SIMON & SCHUSTER BOOKS FOR YOUNG READERS is a trademark of

Simon & Schuster, Inc. For information about special discounts for bulk purchases, please contact

Simon & Schuster Special Sales at 1-866-506-1949 or business@simonandschuster.com.

The Simon & Schuster Speakers Bureau can bring authors to your live event.

For more information or to book an event, contact the Simon & Schuster Speakers Bureau

at 1-866-248-3049 or visit our website at www.simonspeakers.com.

Book design by Lizzy Bromley • The text for this book was set in Centaur. • The illustrations for this book were

rendered in acrylics, colored pencils, and opaque inks on Arches watercolor paper. • Manufactured in China

0719 SCP • First Edition • 2 4 6 8 10 9 7 5 3 1 • Library of Congress Cataloging-in-Publication Data

Names: Johnston, Tony, 1942– author. | LaMarche, Jim, illustrator. • Title: Puma dreams / Tony Johnston ; illustrated

by Jim LaMarche. • Description: First edition. | New York : Simon & Schuster Books for Young Readers, [2019] |

"A Paula Wiseman Book." | Summary: A young girl yearns to see an elusive puma in the wild, knowing that their

numbers are dwindling and that what her Gram calls a "long-dream" may never come true.

Identifiers: LCCN 2019000341 | • ISBN 9781534429796 (hardcover) | ISBN 9781534429802 (eBook)

Subjects: | CYAC: Dreams—Fiction. | Grandmothers—Fiction. | Puma—Fiction. | Endangered species—Fiction.

Classification: LCC PZ7.J6478 Pum 2019 | DDC [E]—dc23

LC record available at https://lccn.loc.gov/2019000341